Halloween In The City With A Real One

D'Artanya

"Did you go pay the rent yet?" India called me from work for the second time today.

"Nah, I'mma get up and go soon." I was stuck on the couch, legs stretched, hands on my sack. I smashed two plates of leftovers after doming a whole blunt to the face. A nigga wasn't getting up to do shit except get in the bed.

I had our son, Jelani, knocked out on my chest. That's my lil man. I worked nights while India worked days. I worked Thursday-Monday. She worked Monday through Friday, so we didn't get much time together. But we were working so we could. Grinding now to shine later. Right now, it was some bullshit, but we were doing what we had to do.

"I have a few hours of sick time left, I'll just come home early and take it to the rental office."

"I got it, Dia. I'm gonna pay it. Our son is sleeping, anyway. Relax, you get to leaving early and then when your check come in, you gon' blame me." I laughed.

"You right. Just take it as soon as Jelani wakes up, please," she begged.

"I'm on it."

"Ok, well I'll see you when I get home. Love you."

"I love you, too."

I stared at the clock on the wall. The ticks were the loudest thing in the room. I was stalling, I was scared as shit to run into

Dre. We bet on the game Sunday. I put my half of the rent money on the Ravens, just for them to lose it all to a kick. It was a verbal bet with a promise to pay Monday morning. It was Monday morning and Dre took his bets seriously, verbal or otherwise. I knew when I made the bet that I would take the ass whooping if I loss.

If I could avoid that nigga for two days, I could pay the rent and give him his cash. India was still going to swing on me when she found out I bet that much on a game. It'd be worse if I didn't pay the rent. This shit might've been the icing on the cake.

When Jelani woke up, I bundled him into a thick Nike onesie and a Nike snow jacket and put him in the stroller. I took a few peeks out the window before carrying the stroller down the front steps.

I kept my eyes forward as I walked to the rental office. Dre was nowhere in sight. I dug in my pockets to grab the money order but pulled out cash instead. I'd forgotten I was supposed to get a money order first.

"Fuck!"

I stared at Jelani's stroller. I could get there and back faster if I just carried him. The quicker I moved the less likely I was to run into Dre. But if I did run into him, lil man was his safest in his stroller. "Fuck it." I mumbled, bopping off to the check cashing spot.

Waiting in the long ass line, my palms began to sweat.

"You see them bum ass Ravens last night?" I jumped at the voice I heard making conversation.

Turning, I saw it was just a random dude behind me. Everyone sounded like Dre as scared as I was.

"Yeah, man. I saw that bullshit." I shook my head, turning back around.

"I lost a lot of money on that game, man." He was still talking.

"Tell me about it."

When I finally made it to the counter, money in hand ready to pay, Jelani started to fuss. I put his pacifier in his mouth to quiet him while I got my money order.

"I don't need a money order, cash is fine." I looked up to Dre snatching the money from my hand.

"It's all there, man." Watching him counting my rent money pissed me off.

"I believe you, but I gotta be sure." Dre continued counting.

"Sir, do you need help or not? You holding the line up," the cashier threw her arms up.

"You got a couch that I can sleep on?" I asked, seriously. I knew I needed somewhere to stay tonight because India was putting me out.

"Boy, get the fuck," she pointed me out of the spot.

"Nice doing business with you," Dre smiled, holding the door open for me and the stroller. "You wanna bet on Sunday's game?"

"Fuck no, nigga."

Dre laughed, walking off.

I sat on the bus stop to feed a crying Jelani. I had to figure something out. We were two months behind, and this payment would've gotten us caught up. I fucked that all up. We wouldn't be evicted but we were supposed to renew our lease next month. The landlord warned us that if we were late again, we wouldn't be granted the renewal option. India was going to kill me.

After burping Jelani, I strapped him back in the stroller and walked to my mother's house. She was my only way out of it. I only needed to borrow the money for two days. I reached for my key only to remember that my mother took my key. I knocked on the door repeatedly until she answered.

"What boy, why you knocking on my fucking door like that?" she mugged me and immediately put a smile on her face to greet Jelani. "Hi, grandma's baby." She pulled him from the stroller. "Your daddy thinks I'm finna babysit, but I'm not." She kissed his face. "No, I'm not," she sang to him.

"Nah," I scratched the back of my neck.

"What you want? More money? I don't have it." She moved her hand in the infamous "period" gesture.

"It's for the rent, Ma. I fucked up." I ran my hands down my face.

"Nothing new." She mumbled. "I don't have it, Rari. You already owe me seven hundred dollars, Rari." Her hands shook near her face. "When you gonna stop fucking up, huh? I'm done saving you. I'm sorry. If y'all need to come on here, fine but I'm done paying your bills and mine. Because if I keep paying y'alls bills, I'm going to get put out of my shit, too."

"Aight. Give me my son," I snatched Jelani from her arms.

"I'll see you later grandma's baby. Ya daddy got an attitude," she antagonized. I didn't expect anything less. All my life, she was the mother that wanted to tit for tat. When I got old enough to take an ass whooping, I was barely home. She didn't care because she was barely home. She wasn't fiend out or anything like that she just partied hard.

"You won't. If you can't help us, you can't see him." I carried the stroller down the steps of the porch to the sidewalk.

"You ain't hurting nobody but yourself, boy. You gon eat them words. You hear me?"

"Yeah, I'm gon' eat real good from your inheritance when

you outta here. Then, I'll get everything I deserved from day one."

"Bitch, I will write you out the Will right the fuck now. Play with me."

I ignored her and kept walking, pushing Jelani's stroller. If she had set me up to be financially responsible, I wouldn't be in this predicament. I was serious bout what I said to her. I was gon' get myself out of this bind and I wasn't fucking with her no more.

She never acknowledged that I was trying. I'd been working this job for three solid months and hadn't been late once. And I was taking the bus to and from so that was a big deal. Yeah, I owed her seven hundred, but I had already paid back a thousand. I was fucking trying.

Back at home, I put Jelani into her bouncer while I made dinner. Fried chicken, corn from the can and some boxed mac and cheese; nothing fancy. I wasn't a world star chef, but I knew enough to feed my family. We weren't gon' go hungry around this bitch.

After I ate and gave Jelani a bath, we fell asleep in the bedroom. I woke up to my work alarm going off and India shoving me.

"Wake up, bae."

"I'm up," I mumbled not wanting to talk, let alone get up and ready for work.

"You paid the rent, right?"

That made me jump up. I began rushing around to get out of there. I wasn't ready to have that conversation.

"Rari." India sucked her teeth. "Please tell me you paid the rent." She touched her hands to her temple.

I couldn't even say the shit to her. I ran my hands down my face. "Look, I'mma get it paid, Dia. I promise. I owed Dre—" she didn't even let me finish.

"You always owe somebody." She threw her hands up and shook them as if her hands were around my neck. "What about what you owe us? Me and Jelani. When are you going to start paying back what you owe us?" She would've been yelling if Jelani wasn't sleep.

"I do my part. I cook, I help clean, I help with Jelani more than any other nigga helps with their child. The married bitches at work complain the entire ten-hour shift about how they have to go home and still do A, B, and C when they get home." I was offended. I was fucking up, but I was doing my part as a father. I was killing this man of the house shit.

"I don't care about nobody but the people in *this* house. Fuck your coworkers, Rari. It's just one fuck up after the other, I'm tired. Our lease is up in a month, now we have to move. You got somewhere for us to go?" She raised her eyebrows at me.

"Say what you want, but don't I always figure it out? Since Jelani got here, it's like you doubting me and shit. It don't fucking feel good, Dia. I'm trying but shit like this, make me feel like it's never enough."

"It's not." She was off the bed punching her fist into her palm. "I had enough faith in you for me. I allowed you to show up for me as you could figuring one day, you'd get it right. Ain't no more one days, Rari. Jelani is here and you gotta come harder, my nigga. Better than this."

"That's fucked up!" I yelled.

Jelani started crying and it bought the both of us back to reality.

"There you go again, disrupting routines." India put Jelani to her breast.

"That's my bad. You want me to stay so I can put him back to sleep?"

"No, just go to work. We need the money." Her eyes were watering, and I wasn't going to stay and watch her cry. I felt fucked up enough.

"Aight, see you in the morning."

I left out through the back door not wanting to waste any time with all the niggas out front standing around. I waited around at the bus stop for what felt like forever. It was only ten minutes, but my mind was heavy. In the heat of the moment, I was in my feelings but riding the bus with nothing to do but think, the only thing on my mind was Dia's words. I fucked up.

Being off the bus, I noticed a scratch off left on the seat. Didn't look like it belonged to anyone on the bus, so I grabbed it. The bus stop wasn't but a block away from the job. I put the scratch off in my pocket to save it for break. I talked to Dia for my first break, but I doubt she was going to want to talk to me later.

I clocked in, put on the new Gates, and jumped right into my work. My first break wasn't until twelve. At 11:55 PM my boss met me on my lift truck and asked me to come to his office. This was the conversation I'd been waiting to have. I was finishing up on my ninety-day probation period and couldn't stop smiling knowing that I had some good news to take home to India. It wouldn't fix shit, but it gave us something to look forward to.

Do you know these niggas let me work for four hours just to fire me? Some bullshit bout not hitting my numbers to be a full time associate. It was bullshit. My numbers weren't the best, but I was bringing them up every week. I was counting on that five dollar raise we got after making it permanent. I wasn't going home with more bad news for India.

I made it two steps out of work before it started pouring down.

Tired wasn't the fucking word. I'd woken up after a five-hour nap and was still tired. This was the first weekend I had off in months. I worked as much as I could because I didn't have shit else to do. But this weekend, I was planning on staying in the house until Halloween was over. I was not for the shit this year.

After seven years of this new life, I was over it. If this was how it had to be, then so be it. I wasn't doing the shit anymore. I preferred it this way. I hated people and how selfish they were. It was best that I'd be left alone. Work and home; that is my life now. Oh, and books. I love books.

My long nap session came with more sweat than I could handle. I took a long shower before slipping into my favorite nighties. Cookies, wine, and a good book would be my company for the weekend.

I danced my way into the kitchen, I could taste the chocolate chip cookies already. I opened the fridge, and my heart sank. The cookies were gone. I pulled the wine bottle from the fridge and could feel it wasn't enough for even a half glass of wine. I had a solid thirty minutes before it was officially Halloween. I could run to the store and make it back by then.

I rushed into my bedroom and tossed on the first pair of socks I saw. One was black and the other was white. It never mattered what I wore, no one would notice. I threw on some sweats, and a hoodie, tossed on my bonnet and my beat up Timbs and then made it out the door with twenty-five minutes to make it back home.

Getting my car from the parking garage would take too much time, so I used my feet to get me there. In my other life, I ran track for my high school. I ran the 300-and 400-meter hurdles and always came in first place. I'm this life, I smoked cigarettes and weighed close to two hundred pounds mostly due to the wine and cookies.

I got outside to see that it was pouring down. I ran back inside climbing the wooden steps two at a time. I tossed my bonnet on and searched around for my umbrella. Unable to find it or spend any more time on it, I gave up. I could be wet for a few minutes.

Entering the liquor store, I could see the line was empty. I rushed to grab my wine from the fridge because I could get cookies at the register. I grabbed a bottle of Taylor Port, then doubled back and grabbed another, just to be safe. When I turned the line was full. Ten people in total but it looked like at least seven transactions.

I checked my watch, and I was down to ten minutes. It was fine, I could wait. If worse came to worse, I could just avoid everyone until I was safe inside my apartment.

The line was moving fast until the customer before me decided to split his payment between two cards and some cash. I watched the clock strike twelve as the cashier handed him his change. My heart began to race. I could feel beads of sweat forming on my forehead. It was hot. It felt like everyone's eyes were on me.

"Ma'am, go the fuck head, damn!" the customer behind me snapped.

"Oh, I'm sorry." I shook my head taking a deep swallow as I walked up to the register.

I placed my wine bottles on the counter before snatching a pack of cookies from their place on the mini hook. When the cashier told me the price, I dug in my pocket for my bank card. It wasn't there. I hadn't grabbed it when I rushed out of the house.

"Man, fuck it. I'll pay for it, just take it." The customer behind me was fed up with my shit.

"No! I don't want it. I'll just go home and get my card. Thank you." I told the cashier before mean mugging the bastard that offered to pay.

"Bitch, I was tryna be nice to yo' homeless ass."

I walked backwards towards the door. "And I bet you still want a piece of this pussy." I tapped my hand against my pussy. I felt a cold breeze hit my back and immediately turned around to see a man holding the door for me. I froze in fear.

"Fuck is you doing?" he asked.

"I don't need you to hold the door for me, nigga. I got hands." I held my hands up to him.

"Well, get the fuck out my way," he pulled me by the arm, yanking me out of the store so he could walk inside. "Weird as bitch," he mumbled.

"No, no, no, no." I paced outside of the store. I looked up to see a passerby whispering and a few people on their phones just waiting for me to do something worthy of going viral. I leaned against the wall of the liquor store lifting one foot behind me, hitting my head gently against the cold, red, bricks.

That wasn't a favor, was it? Like technically, he was being rude. He wasn't helping me, right? Fuck. I just had to be a glutton and get my wine and cookies. I should've stayed in the fucking house. I walked in the direction of home to see how far I could get away from him. I made it to one corner before I was stuck like a mouse on a mouse trap.

I saw the nigga that couldn't keep his hands to himself walking out of the store with a smile on his face.

"You stupid nigga!" I walked over to him.

"Bitch, go head," he walked in the opposite direction.

I picked up my pace, damn near running to catch up to him.

"You have no idea what you've just done," I turned the corner he turned.

"I opened the door for you. Why the fuck is you tripping, girl?" We crossed the street together.

"You've never heard the saying 'no good deed goes unpunished'? Yeah, well, here I am in the fucking flesh. This shit is so dumb!" I screamed.

"You on some weird shit. I don't hit women, but I'll slam you on your neck, bitch. Stop fucking following me," he pointed in my face.

"Boy, please. I'd rather be in my fucking apartment, minding my gotdamn business until this horrid weekend is over!" I yelled in his face.

Next thing I knew, I was pinned to the bricks of a building with his hands around my throat.

"Look, bitch. I'm having a long fucking day. Leave me the fuck alone!" he barked in my face before walking away.

"I can't because you held the fucking door open for me!"

Frustrated wasn't the word. My head pounded and my stomach turned. It took everything in me not to cry in front of this nigga. God, I hated this holiday. I hated this fucking life. I wanted to be free of this shit.

"Here." He walked back to me, opened the building door, and pushed me inside. He slammed in it in my face. "You happy now? Go the fuck head, bitch, damn!" he yelled at me.

"Cute, but it's too late. I owe you three fucking wishes. Let's go, I don't have all night. You have until twelve am to get these wishes up off me. If you don't make them, I make them for you."

His nose wrinkled as he tilted his head to the side. I think he wanted to believe me but the hood in him wouldn't allow him. The only thing we believed in that we couldn't see was God, everything else was fake until proven otherwise. He looked at his watch.

"Oh, you taking this Halloween shit to a whole other level. Find someone else to perform for. I'm not interested." He shook his head, trying to walk away from me. I followed.

"I'm serious. I know it sounds like some bullshit but I'm a genie." I exhaled, giving up on being angry.

The convincing was always the longest part. A lot of Halloween was wasted on trying to convince these humans that I could make their dreams come true.

"Bitch, please. You look homeless."

"That's on purpose. I didn't want anyone to notice me in case I was outside once the clock struck twelve. I was just making a quick store run." I shook my head.

"You are in full character." He laughed.

I stopped in front of a playground and gave him my best shot. "Your name is Wayne Hall. You go by Rari. Your mother used to call you Wayne and over time you were left with just Rari. It fits you." I sat at a bench in front of the park. "Your fast, always on the move. But you're also smooth. Since Jelani got here, you less fast and more smooth but still." I shrugged.

"What the fuck?" he joined me on the bench.

"Yeah, I know all your business. Your flaws, too. You're indecisive, impatient, you're impulsive-"

"Man, fuck all that. Do a trick."

"Bitch, I'm not a dog." I sucked my teeth.

"Aye, Genie or not. You call me another bitch and you gon' have to square up."

"You just called me 50-11 bitches." I twisted my lips.

"And I'm sorry." He made eye contact. "Just having a bad day, my bad. Look, we can start over, my name is Rari. Nice to meet you," he held his hand out to me.

"Misiria."

"That's different," his voice glazed over, and his shoulders lowered.

It usually took longer for them to hear the misery in Misiria. I'd say my name upon meeting them and typically never needed to say it again. But when misery came, they suddenly asked my name again.

Rari knew the moment it left my lips, I didn't want to talk about how I was misery in the flesh. So, I gave him a small nod confirming his quiet thoughts.

"Nothing in life is free, but I guess I can prove myself." I focused my attention back on the task.

"Well, I'm waiting." Rari threw his arms up.

"Cover your ears."

"Huh?"

"*Huh?*" I mocked him. "Cover your ears, fam." I sucked my teeth.

"Childish." He stuck his fingers inside his ears.

"Who covers their ears like that?" I twisted my neck at him.

"A nigga with common sense. You gon' do the trick or not? Damn."

I blinked and all six traffic lights turned green. Horns honked and tires skid. Then, all six cars crashed into one another.

"I said do a trick, not kill people," Rari stood with his hands on his head and his pants sagging.

His medium T-shirt lifted with his arms and his pelvic line showed. The little hair going up to his navel was jet black against his smooth skin. Getting caught in the rain, made his shirt cling to his chest. The exposed droplets that sat on his skin, glistened under the streetlights.

"Relax, no one died."

"They could've. Let's get out of here, shit mad uncomfortable. I feel like I did something wrong." Rari led the way.

"Aight, aight." He twisted his head once we bent the corner. "So, how this shit work?" We found an apartment awning to stand under.

"Well, you get three wishes. I grant them. If you are not making your wishes quick enough, I make them for you. You do not want me to make them for you."

"What happens if you make them?" he asked.

"So, if you make at least two, you're good. But If I have to make two of your wishes for you, I decide your fate at the end of the night."

"My fate?"

"Yeah," I nodded. I wasn't anywhere near ready for that part of the night. It could take its time. "So, I can't go too far from you. Like, when you were in the liquor store, I could only go as far as the other corner. We're basically tied at the hip until the clock strikes twelve."

"I can't go home with some chick on my arm. My girl will kill me." Rari stood, panicked.

"Well, she thinks you are at work, right?" I began walking

from under the awning. "We can go to my place until we figure something out."

"Damn, I thought you were homeless." Rari looked honestly shocked.

"Boy, fuck you. Oh, and I need wine and cookies." I walked us back into the direction of the liquor store.

Rari laughed. I was certain that I wouldn't hear that for the rest of the day. That laugh would turn into tears soon. He didn't even see it coming.

None of this shit made sense to me. My focus was on not going home, so if this bitch wanted to pretend to be a genie for Halloween, cool. As long as I didn't have to go home and tell India that I lost my job. If I could get my lie off for a few days until I found another job, I'd be straight. I needed the time to think of some bullshit to tell her.

"Damn, you could've held the door for me." She sucked her teeth, letting go of the door.

"Last time I did that, you went the fuck off on me." I eyed her, allowing her to lead us to her place.

"It doesn't matter anymore. You already did the favor. You're stuck with me until this is over."

"Why you keep saying shit like that? Stuck? Talking about good deed not going unpunished, what's up?" I asked curious as to what was really going on. It was sounding like these wishes were bad things.

"Just that people think they want something, until they get it and can't get rid of it." She stared off.

It looked like she was about to cry. I couldn't take seeing women cry, so I changed the subject.

"So, if Genie's exist, what else is out there that people like me think is fake?" I drank some of the orange juice I grabbed when we doubled back to the liquor store.

"I don't know. I don't even know if Genies exist per se. I just know that I'm one." She shrugged. "There's definitely other people with gifts out there but I never cared to ask."

"Then, how can you know?"

"Because sometimes when I'm out, they notice me. They say excuse me or pass me a smile. More often I get the pity look like they know my curse."

"I noticed you so I must have a gift." I tapped my chest.

"No." She laughed at me. "You noticed me because it's Halloween. It's the only time people pay me any real attention." She pulled a door handle to what looked like a hotel suite.

"Damn, this where you live. So, what you rich or something?

"I work. It's all I do." We stepped onto the elevator. "It's not like I have shit else to do. I told you. People don't see me."

"So, you just invisible the other 364 days of the year?" I asked.

"Pretty much. I'm that person at work no one notices. They see me, but like it's like I'm not there. They don't acknowledge me. I guess that's a better way to put it."

"Damn." We stepped off the elevator and walked a hall to what I assumed was her apartment.

"Yeah, I know. I still have to work because I still have to take care of myself. I still have to sleep and shit like normal people."

"What about sex?" It may have been forward, but I was curious. She froze with her key in the lock. "My bad if that's too personal, but since you read my whole life back to me, I figured we were well acquainted." I shrugged.

She cleared her throat while opening the door to her place.

"Um, I mean," I watched her take a hard swallow. "Like I said, no one notices me."

"Right."

Her apartment was nice. A soft pink sofa that stretched the

length of the wall. A rectangular shaped coffee table, studded in rhinestones at the base. Mirrors lined every wall and a single photo in a frame sat on the shelf under the TV. I only noticed it because she slammed it down. I figured she didn't want me to see it.

"What time do you usually get off work?" she asked.

"Six."

We both looked down at our watches. I had a little over five hours before I had to be home.

"Cool. Well, the bathroom is down the hall to the left if you need to use the bathroom or shower or something."

"Bet." I went to take a seat on the sofa.

"I should've said that a shower wasn't optional. You can take a shower or stand. I want my place as dirt free as possible."

"Aight." I threw my arms up. "You got some shit I can toss on when I get out?"

"Um, yeah. I'll have something ready for you."

"Cool." I walked off to the bathroom.

It felt like we were vibing a little, until I asked about sex. She couldn't hide that she was uncomfortable. I wasn't tryna fuck, I loved India. I was just curious as to how her needs changed with being a Genie and shit.

I stepped out of the shower to find clothes on the counter. The shit looked familiar. I examined the clothes while drying my dick to see they were mine. Like, the shit I had on the day before was right in front of me. I tossed the clothes on and rushed out of the bathroom. This genie bitch was interesting.

I came out the bathroom to her in a different t-shirt, curled up on the couch under a whole blanket. She looked comfortable.

"You know, you could've at least grabbed clean clothes. This shit is from my hamper." I shook my head, taking a seat next to her. "What you got bad magic or something?"

"You get what you get, and you don't throw a fit," she sparked a blunt. "So, what's your first wish?" She leaned back against the couch.

"I ain't too sure about all this wish shit." I hit one fist into my palm, legs spread on the couch.

"My nigga. What else do I have to do to prove that I am who I say I am?" she passed me the blunt.

"Ain't no glitter or no extra shit in here, right?" I looked at it.

"Smoke it or don't, yo'," she rolled her eyes.

I put it to my lips, and it taste like grape. Like, maybe she'd eaten a Now and Later or wore grape scented gloss. I stared at her lips wondering if maybe she just tasted like grapes. I was drawn to this chick. It could've been the magic of the night but whatever it was, I liked it.

"What the fuck are you looking at?" She snatched the blunt from my hands. "Ain't gonna be none of that humping and thumping, shit. Just make your wishes and go."

"Damn. I ain't said shit about having sex with you. Must be on your mind."

"Whatever. Make a wish."

"I ain't feeling it." I clapped my hands together. "You don't look like you're having fun. My grandmother always told me not to be dibbling and dabbling with spiritual gifts and all that. It doesn't seem worth the wish, no matter how bad I want it."

Misiria tilted her head slightly with a softer gaze than I'd received all night. Her eyes glistened in the light. I don't know what I said or how she was feeling about it, but the energy changed. It was warm when it'd been cold. Inviting, when she'd rejected me every chance she got.

"I said something good?" I asked, curious.

"What make you think that?" She readjusted on the couch. Her back leaned against the arm of the chair, with one leg up. Comfortable.

"Beside the fact that you're stuck? You've had a comeback all night and now, nothing? The entire room warmed up like the middle of a summer day. I didn't know you could change the temperature in a room. And it's like mustard yellow. That shit is weird by the way." I told her before snatching the blunt from her.

"Nah." She cleared her throat. "My energy big. Bold. Domineering. Everything within fifteen feet of me gets wrapped up in my energy. So, the room didn't warm, technically. I did."

We stared at one another as I moved closer to her. I wanted to tell her that I liked it. She could wrap me as tight as she wanted in her energy. Shit made my dick tingle.

"What's your wish?"

"What's off limits?" I asked, looking in between her thighs before finding her eyes. They were glued to me. I watched her take a hard swallow.

"I can't make you rich, fam. I can't bring anyone back from the dead. Unlike the typical genie story, I *can* make two people fall in love. But, only if they're meant to be."

"Who's the judge on what's meant to be and what ain't?"

"The universe. God. Or whoever you believe in. Whatever you believe in, also believes in balance. When two people who are not meant to be together, get together, it causes a disturbance to every person they know. Something changes rather it be pulling them away from the person they're supposed to be with, or I don't know, anything. It basically messes up the flow of things."

"Man, this shit is wild." I ran my hand through my fade. "Um, a stable job. I don't care what it is I just want to provide for my family."

"Ok." She looked up to the sky. "Universe, give him what he asks for." Misiria gave me a sad smile.

My stomach turned. This night was crazy. I didn't understand anything that was going on. I still had two wishes left, the night was just getting started.

"Why it feel like outside now? Cold and damp and blue." Rari got up changing the temp on the thermostat. "What you sad about?"

"Nothing." I put my knees to my chest and rested my head atop.

I didn't know what was about to happen. I was nervous.

"So, where's my new job at, fam? Your magic broke or something?"

"No, stupid. It's already done." I rolled my eyes.

"Well, how long we gotta wait for?"

"I don't know. We can do something, it's Halloween. I'm sure its hella scary movies playing." I turned on the TV to find us something scary to watch. I didn't care what it was honestly, I just wanted to distract myself from him. He was fine as fuck.

I chose The First Purge. The one with the black people. It was the best one of all the sequels.

"Why you put this bullshit on?" Rari asked.

"What? Boy, please. This shit fire." Of course, he had bad taste in movies. Something had to be wrong with his perfect ass.

"Nah, it's cool or whatever but I hate that romantic shit in a horror movie. Like, if a nigga tryna kill me, I promise you, pussy is the last thing on my mind. A nigga tryna make it home, you feel me. All the love interest do, is hold the hero. Every time. She always fucks up some kind of way. Heroes never leave the girl and that shit ain't realistic because unless we got some time in, I'm leaving your ass."

"When you going through some shit like this you only need one person that's gon' hold you down. If you loyal, you both make it out. The motherfucker trying to save himself and no one else always dies."

"That's true. So, if Halloween gets crazy, you gone hold me down?" Rari looked to me with soft eyes.

My body warmed at the question. I wanted to say fuck yeah but if he was joking, I'd die of embarrassment.

"The room is red and hot. Yeah, you definitely want a nigga. I know I said that shit was weird earlier but I'm starting to think its sexy as fuck." Rari leaned into me, and I froze. I closed my eyes and my pussy thumped anticipating his kiss. We were interrupted by his phone chiming.

"Good luck." I whispered, sitting back against the couch.

I wasn't sure if my heart raced because of the moment Rari and I had just shared or because I was scared for him. That email could say anything. I watched his eyes scan through the email.

"I'm actually not mad about this."

"Is that your wish? The job?" I asked, not understanding why he wasn't upset.

"Yeah, I'm being offered a manager position at McDonalds."

"Congratulations. If you like it, I love it."

"Thank you." Rari looked to me with a sincere smile on his face. "I needed this for my family."

His family. I almost forgot he had one. Out of sight, out of mind, I guess. He was just trying to kiss me two seconds ago.

"You're welcome, I guess." I turned the movie up, rolling my eyes.

"What's your problem?" he asked me.

"Nothing. I just want to watch the movie."

"You lying. The room is green and smells like charcoal. And it's cold again," he snatched some of my covers and got comfortable under them. "What's wrong?"

I gave him my attention but still didn't speak, I just stared at him. He turned the TV one and adjusted his body to face me.

"You jealous."

I looked away from him. "I think we should just focus our attention on your wishes."

He was right, I was jealous. I wanted to be someone's family. It didn't have to be Rari's, I just wanted to belong to someone like him. Someone that would always have me on their mind.

"I'm not trying to lead you on. I don't really know what's going on with that part. I love my girl, but something is drawing me too you. I don't know if it's the magic, but I like you."

I tried not to smile but it was plastered on my face like a fat kid in front of a piece of cake. "I like you, too."

"But, if I'm being honest, I don't want to. I can't fuck up anymore with my girl. If she were to leave me, I don't know what a nigga would do. So, I think you're right. We should focus on these wishes."

"Right." I cleared my throat. "What's your second wish?" I asked unconcerned, watching the movie.

"Please, don't be like that. We were having a good time. We can still be cool as shit after all this."

The problem was that he wouldn't remember after this. I'd never forget him, but he'd forget I ever existed. He'd moved on with his life and the small footprints I left made in his world would be erased.

"What's your second wish." I stared blankly at him as if his words had no effect on me.

"You said you can't make me rich, right?"

"Correct."

"Can you get me a lot of money, though?"

"I can." I nodded, getting up. I walked over to the window and pulled the curtains. I focused on a star. "Universe, do your thing," I said, before taking a seat back on the sofa.

"And now we wait," Rari said.

I ignored him. It wasn't long before I was being a creep and watching him sleep. I know I didn't have the right to be upset but the shit hurt. It wasn't fair. The one time I get to help someone I'm attracted to and he's madly in love with a woman that probably doesn't deserve him. I didn't know if that was true or not because I only had details about Rari, but I knew how I could find out.

"Wake up," I shoved his head straight.

"What time is it? My wish here?" He looked around and felt inside his pockets.

"No. It's time for you to go home." I pointed to the clock showing that it was the time he used to get off work.

He stretched and yawned before standing from the couch. "You ready?"

"Yup. We can take my car." I shoved my current read into my purse.

"What you bringing that for?" I asked.

"I need something to do while you get rid of your girlfriend." I shrugged.

I did all the walking I was going to do for the day. Plus, Rari lived a good thirty minutes away. That was more than an hour by foot.

"Nice car," Rari said, getting into the passenger seat.

"Thank you."

"You gon' need to fix your attitude before we get to my crib. Whatever you feeling for me got to go. My girl can smell that shit on other women. I don't have time for that shit today."

"Excuse me?" I stopped at the stop sign and put my car in park.

"This shit right here. I don't have time for it. I come home the same time every day. If I'm even a few minutes late, she knows something is up. Drive this motherfucker, yo'."

"Who are you talking to?" I asked.

"Ain't nobody else in here." He looked around the car. "Drive this motherfucker, yo'."

"You could make your last wish and walk your ass home. We don't have to be tied together for another fucking second. Do it! Make your stank ass wish." I glared at him.

"Calm the fuck down." he shook his head.

"I am calm."

"Bullshit. The car is so damn red, I can barely see out the fucking window," he pointed.

"I can see just fine. Sounds like a *you* problem."

"And it smells like a fire in here." He rolled down the window to cough. "Relax."

Rari had pissed me off, but I didn't want to kill him from smoke inhalation, so I calmed myself down. He hadn't done anything wrong. I was the one who got my hopes up, knowing this could only end in one of two ways. Neither of those ways would allow us to be together so I was being extra.

"Why my wish gotta be stank?" he twisted his neck at me.

I couldn't help but to burst into laughter. "Let's get you home, clown."

"Thank you." He threw his arms up. "That's all I asked for."

We rode the rest of the way to his house in silence. I guessed we were both in our heads. My mind raced trying to think of all the ways his wish for money could go wrong. That was a waste of time because it wasn't like I could narrow it down or some shit. I'd just have to wait and see like him. Whatever it was, I knew it would end this little friendship for good.

"Aight. So, my girl is moving around getting ready for work. When she leaves you can come in."

"Cool," Misiria nodded, never looking up from her phone.

I knew she was only trying to avoid eye contact because the space turned grey and smelled of charcoal.

"I know this shit is uncomfortable. It's almost over." She still didn't look up from her phone.

I felt bad. She was cool. I genuinely liked her. India was my everything, though. I'd done enough fucking up. It was time to step up for her, no matter how attracted I was to Misiria.

I walked in the door to see Dia dressed and ready for work. She had Jelani feeding from her breast. While the other hand clung tightly to her phone.

"What's up?" I asked, walking in.

"Hey."

I walked over trying to give her a kiss and she moved her face.

"Oh, you still got an attitude. Cool."

"Your mom is supposed to be stopping by with Jelani's costume." She pulled Jelani from her breast and passed him to me. "Well, that was before you cursed her out yesterday."

"So, you mad about that now, too?"

"Because why do you insist on arguing with her all the time?

Sometimes you can just be quiet."

"I been doing that all my life! Stop commenting on my relationship with my mother. You don't know who she used to be."

"I know who she is now and she's helpful. She cares about Jelani. I don't know if you're jealous but—"

"Jealous of my son?" I twisted my neck. "Take ya' goofy ass to work, man. It don't have shit to do with him. My issue with my mother is my issue with my mother. I keep telling you to mind your business. Now you all upset, and my mother and I will be fine. We always are."

"Please, Rari. When she stops by, at least grab Jelani's costume before you send her off."

"You don't even be listening. I just said we good."

"But, is the rent good?"

"Here you go." I threw my arms up. "I get paid tomorrow. I'm going to pay the shit, man."

"And the security deposit and first month rent for the new place?"

I lowered my shoulders, defeated.

"That's what I thought. Please have Jelani ready to go trick or treating when I get home." India walked out of the door without another look in my direction.

I missed the sweet parts of her. India had been cold towards me since having Jelani. Even with me getting the stability she asked for. She didn't trust me, and I could feel it. For real, for real it made a nigga not want to come home. But I was there. Work and home that's all I did. I don't even remember the last time I was outside kicking it with my niggas.

I watched India from the window. Misiria leaned against the tree with the book she refused to leave in the house. She never lifted her head until India was unable to see her face. I watched the color change from yellow, to orange, to a dull ass Khaki color. I couldn't feel her but the expression on her face was confusion.

Misiria stared at India's car until she was out of view, and I stared at Misiria. She looked up at the window and we both rushed to look away. I walked over to the door to let her in.

"What's wrong?"

"Nothing." The color around her faded.

"Well, go around back. I don't need nobody running back to India to tell her I was bringing some bitch in our house." Misria cut her eyes at me. "Their words, not mine." I held my hand to my chest.

"Whatever." Misria headed around back.

Jelani started crying as I shut the front door. I scooped him into my arms, rocking him as we walked to the back door to let Misiria in. When I opened the door, she was just walking up the steps.

"He's so handsome." Misiria stopped to smile at my son.

"Handsome and cold, hurry up so I can shut the door." I rushed her.

"Oh, sorry." She quickly made her way up the steps.

"You good." I shut the back door. "And thank you. He gets his looks from me." I smirked.

"That's obvious." She took a seat on the couch, pulling her book out.

"Hold up, you tryna say my girl ugly?" I twisted my lips.

"Hey, you said it not me," she shrugged.

"That's fucked up." I sat next to her on the couch.

I rocked Jelani to sleep on my chest, watching ESPN while

Misiria read her book quietly. Here and there she'd burst into laughter, and I'd be lying if I said I was a little interested in what she was reading. When I went to lay Jelani down, I smelled poop.

"Fuck," I whispered.

I laid him on the couch to change his diaper and the doorbell rang. "Give me a second!" I called out, waking Jelani up, fussing.

"Here," Misiria put her book down. "I'll take care of him, and you can get the door." She stood, pushing me out of the way.

She distracted him with a few tickles that had him laughing like tickle me Elmo.

I opened the door to see a police officer at the door. A pool of water sat at the rim of his eyelid, threatening to spill over like a full cup.

"I'm looking for Wayne Hall."

My chest thumped. I felt sick. I knew I hadn't committed any type of crime. The police could only be at my door for one other reason. My girl or my mother.

"That's me." I cleared my throat.

"I'm here to inform you that your mother was in an accident."

The room spun. The officer's lips moved but I didn't hear anything but loud sirens. I could feel the sirens throughout my body. My chest tightened and I fell to the floor. Everything was blurry but I could see the front door shut.

Misiria put her hand on my head. My body went warm with the room. Slowly, my vision came back, then my hearing. I was wrapped in a soft blue light that felt like I was on a cloud.

"Get the fuck off of me." I pushed her hands.

I rushed around the room to get Jelani's diaper bag together.

I needed to go to the hospital. Seeing her dead on a table would be the only thing that would allow me to believe any of this is real.

"I was just trying to help." She looked around confused.

"Help? All of this is your fault." My arms were stretched in her direction with blame.

"My fault? *You* made the wish my nigga." The room was getting hot and turning red. Misiria was mad but who gave a fuck about that. My mother was dead because of some bullshit as wish she let me make."

"What wish?!"

"For money. That's what you got. Your inheritance."

I forgot that I'd even made that wish. My head was spinning. I held my face trying to stop it, but everything continued moving like I had no say.

"That's not what I asked for!" I grabbed Jelani. "Don't touch him. Don't speak to him. Matter of fact, don't even look at him. This shit is bogus." I walked out of the front door, going over to the neighbor's house.

"Who is it?" Mrs. Dillon asked.

"It's Rari. Can you watch Jelani for a few? I need to run down to the hospital about my mom. I won't be long. I promise." I yelled to a closed door.

The door opened and Mrs. Dillon stood there with a smile. "Of course, I will. Give me that precious baby." She reached for Jelani.

"Thank you. I'll give you a call as soon as I know something."

"Take your time." She nodded, putting his diaper bag on her shoulder before shutting the front door.

"Thanks, again."

I went back over to my place. Misiria was waiting at the front door. She quickly moved when I walked in. I ignored her going to my bedroom to put on clean clothes. Again, when I stepped out of the room, she was right there.

"Why the fuck do you keep following me?" I twisted my neck at her, before pushing past her and going into the living room.

"You know why. I don't have a choice."

"Well, I'm going to the hospital," I moved towards the front door. I opened it and used my hand to usher her out. "Get the fuck out."

I was done being nice. Misiria was a fucked up person. I wanted her the fuck away from me.

"I don't have time for this traffic shit. Can't you just snap your fingers and get us to the fucking hospital." Rari had one hand on his head.

I decided to stop talking to him the moment we left the house. He was angry, he was hurt, and my words wouldn't help anything. It was true that he made the wish, but I made it happen. I hated this part. Everyone put all the blame on me. I just had to sit there and take it because I couldn't reveal the truth of why it happened until after all of the wishes were made.

"No good deed goes unpunished." He wiped his eyes, nodding his head. "All that bullshit you be spitting makes sense now."

"Yea." I nodded my head instead of arguing about whether or not I speak bullshit. He wouldn't hear anything logical anyway.

"Stay the fuck away from me." Rari's eyes were cold as he got out of the car at the stop sign.

He looked at me as if we never shared a connection before slamming the door in my face. To be honest I wasn't surprised with the grief of his wish. I knew that any wish for money would only come from his inheritance. It was the only money that already belonged to him. It was rightfully his.

"I wish I could, but you know the rules." I let him go as far as the magic would allow before it tugged on me to take my foot off the break. I followed behind him in my car, allowing him his space.

This was usually a piece of Halloween that I enjoyed. Victims had a million questions and most times this was when they shut the fuck up. But, I wanted so badly for him to talk to me. I hadn't held a good conversation in years and talking to him was just, I don't know, nice.

After speed walking for twenty minutes, I could see the hospital in the distance. I wasn't surprised that's where we were going. It was the first place I headed when I had my turn. I pulled into a spot in front of the hospital. I got out of the car, using the mobile app to put money on the meter.

"I don't know why the fuck you're still following me," Rari stopped at a bench near the hospital emergency room. He wouldn't even look at me as he spoke.

"I told you. I don't have a choice." I sat on the bench. "Here." I unlaced my tennis shoes, passing him the shoestrings from the sneakers. "Tie me to this bench."

"Bet." Rari didn't hesitate, grabbing the laces.

He tied me to the framing of the bench as tight as he could. He pinched my skin a few times, but I was quiet. A pinch wasn't going to kill me. When I was tied up to his satisfaction, he gave me one final glare before walking through the emergency doors. He made it to check in desk and looked back at me with twisted lips. He thought I was bullshitting until he tried to walk to the elevator doors, and he couldn't go any farther. He could only move towards me. I watched him walk back to me with his head down.

"You believe me now?" It was petty, but I couldn't help it.

He'd been going hard on me, I deserved a turn. It was offensive that he kept questioning who I said I was. This was not some shit I wanted to be. I didn't want to do the shit I did. If it was up to me, I'd be at home with my wine and cookies until this horrid holiday was the fuck over with.

He ignored me while untying me from the bench. I rubbed my wrists as he freed my hands from the laces. I followed him through the hospital door and onto the elevator.

"I'll wait in the waiting area. Give you your privacy." I nodded my head as he walked away.

I had every intention to sit my ass in the waiting room, but my body was trained to follow the pull and my feet followed Rari down the hall. I tried to be as quiet as I could in hopes he wouldn't notice but he did. He shook his head, and I threw my arms up. It was out of my control. If I could stop it, I would.

Rari walked into the room where his mother's body rested, shutting the door behind him. He glanced at me from the window of the door. I sat on the floor off to the side and put my laces back in my sneakers. I patiently waited for any sign of movement. A man walked out of the room, and I knew Rari had finished identifying her body.

I stood from the floor, dusting my hands on the butt of my leggings. I inched my way to the door. It was cracked. I shouldn't have but I listened to Rari's final moments with his mother.

"I'm sorry," he said, barely above a whisper. "If I would've known—" Rari put his fist to his lips before hanging his head low. "Thank you for everything even the shit I fought you on. You did your best and you are the best mother anyone could have." Rari ran his hands down his face, before staring at his mother as if he was waiting for her to move.

I wanted to comfort him. Against his orders for me to leave him the fuck alone, I walked into the room and stretched my arm out to him. As long as he was within fifteen feet of some part of my body, he could feel my energy. The temperature of the room changed to a fall day after a light rain. The grey, dry, dead looking room was filled with reds, oranges, and browns.

"Falls my favorite season." I told him.

"Mine, too. It's beautiful."

Since he was talking. I figured it safe to touch him. I put one hand on his shoulder, trying to give him as much comfort as I could. "I know the calendar starts in January, but I always felt September through November was the time for fresh starts. We shed like the leaves on the trees."

"We can get out of here." Rari gave his mother a kiss on her forehead and led the way out of the hospital.

Outside the sun was starting to set. The roads were still empty. It looked as if there wasn't a storm a few hours ago.

"What time is it?" I looked at my watch.

"Time for me to get my ass home."

"You know you could just rush through your last wish, and it can all be over," I suggested.

It wouldn't be the first time someone had ripped the Band-Aid and caught the Hell waiting for them all at once. Plus, Rari would be in the mood, and I wanted to remember him as the man I was falling for.

"I'm not making any more. So, do what you got to do," Rari said as we got in my car.

I'd heard that one before, too. For some reason, they thought they were doing me some kind of favor by preventing me from fulfilling their wishes. Rari was only hurting himself in the end.

"You have to make your wishes, or I have to make it for you," I warned him.

"More punishments. Those not wishes they're punishments. I don't think it could get much worse so do your thing."

"It's not a punishment. I told you. Balance. The inheritance was the only money that belonged to you. It could only come from that. Anywhere else and it would've thrown everything off. The universe does not revolve around your wants. You asked and you received."

"Received what?!" Rari yelled at me, slapping his hands together.

"What you asked for!" I yelled back, tired of him taking his shit out on me.

"I'm not making no more fucking wishes." Rari turned the heat on in the car.

"Then I guess we'll be stuck together all night because I'm not making them for you!"

I refused. He was already making this my fault. I wasn't going to give him more shit to blame me for. If the three wishes were the end of our journey together, I'd say fuck it. It wasn't. After he made his last wish, we had an even longer road to travel.

I didn't give a fuck what happened. I wasn't making anymore wishes. Misiria and the universe or whoever was responsible could kiss my ass. I wanted out of this game. I didn't want to play anymore. There was no winning. Any wish I made would bring back some bullshit. I wasn't interested in picking the better bullshit between the two. She could pick and I would just deal.

Other than heading home, I didn't know what the fuck to do with myself. My every thought was surrounding my mother. My mind kept replaying my last words to her. It was fucked up. I took my mother out for a few dollars. It didn't matter how much money was in my inheritance it was small shit compared to no longer having a mother.

I couldn't help but to feel like it was Misiria's fault. I know she didn't have that much power, but she didn't even warm me. I know it wouldn't have changed shit, but she could've gave me a heads up. I thought something was happening between us. Like, I felt it. Then she turns and throws this shit on me. I couldn't fuck with her no more. She could put the last wish on me then go about her business. I never wanted to see her again.

We pulled back up to my crib and I didn't even want to let her in. I didn't have much of a choice. I opened the door and nodded for her to go inside. I climbed the railing to grab Jelani from next door.

"That you, Rari?" Mrs. Dillon called out to me behind the closed door.

"Yes ma'am. I'm back."

"Give me a second. I'm coming, baby."

"No problem."

I waited for Mrs. Dillon to come to the door. I looked over at my place and Misiria was in the window, watching them like a fucking cat. She quickly moved when she realized I saw her. "Goofy bitch." I mumbled, hoping she could hear me but knowing she couldn't.

Mrs. Dillon's door opened, and she handed me the baby bag. "Your daddy is here for you." She spoke to Jelani as she gave him a big kiss on his cheek. That's why India hated when I let him with Mrs. Dillon. We'd pick him up and he'd have lipstick all over his face and smell like White Diamonds. I didn't see the harm. She never had kids, so she never had visitors and I knew she'd take good care of Jelani. She always did.

"I hope he didn't do too much fussing." I grabbed him from her arms.

"Not at all. Anytime, you know that," she waved me off.

"Thanks, again." I climbed back over the railing.

"Now, make sure I see my baby in his costume. Dia told me he was going to be a little bumble bee. I can't wait to see him." She smiled wide.

"I got you." I lied, walking into the house.

My stomach turned. We didn't have a costume. My mother never came. What the fuck was I going to tell Dia? That was another thing for her to be pissed with me about. Misiria sat on the couch, reading that damn book as if shit was sweet. I huffed sitting down, wiping all of the lipstick from Jelani's face.

"I told you I wasn't making no more fucking wishes." I barked. "Whose wasting who's time. Tell the universe to do its thing and you can be on your merry fucking way, bitch."

"Bitch?" Misiria twisted her neck at me.

Her eyes did that glossy thing they did. The room went hot and red. I was quick to apologize. "Look, I ain't mean that."

"No, you did. You think this is my fault. You think I enjoy this shit. Poor little *fuck up* Rari has to spend twenty-four hours making three wishes." She mocked me. "I'm stuck like this. I have to spend the rest of my life never being noticed except one day out of the year. Why? Because humans are selfish. I'll never be a wife or a mother. I will never fill love, another person's touch. I won't know peace, ever. Just when I settle with *this* being my life, here you come. I thought you were different."

"I thought you were real. You didn't even warn me."

"I did. I told you no good deed goes unpunished."

"Fuck the riddles, Misiria. You didn't warn me that every wish I made would bring pain."

"I couldn't even if I wanted to. There are certain restrictions. You have to figure it out on your own. I can't tell you that you should feel sad or be angry. If you don't feel it, you don't feel it."

"That's bullshit and you know it."

"I'm serious. I've tried before. I can't even write it down. The pencil will break, catch fire, etc. I am not my own person; I can only do what's allowed," she shrugged.

I was tired of piecing her story together. I wanted the full down. The three wishes couldn't be all there was to it. Something else was waiting for me at the end of all of this.

"What happened to the Genie that captured you?"

"I don't know. All I know is that he remembers me. We'd run into each other randomly and he'd always run out the door before I could say anything to him. Then, one day I just stopped seeing him around. Now that I've been the Genie for a few years, I think he may have left state. Never wanting to lay eyes on me again."

"How'd you become the Genie?"

Before she answered, keys jangled in the lock.

"Oh, no." Misiria whispered before running for the back door.

I walked into the kitchen, knowing she could only be but so far away from me. If I stayed in the kitchen, it should've put me close enough for her to keep her ass outside.

Dia walked in mugging me. She looked around the house like a crazy person.

"What you looking for?" I asked.

"The bitch you got in my house. Don't even try to deny it because by the time lunch hit, I was getting texts, and FB messages from half the block telling me that some bitch was leaving my house."

"And you just coming home to look?" I know I was focused on the wrong shit, but it mattered. The old her would've left work to come see about me and the bitch.

"Yeah, because I really don't give a fuck, Rari. Whoever the bitch is, she can have you. I just wanted the proof, so we didn't have to go back and forth about me putting you out." India walked over snatching Jelani from my arms.

"Putting me out?" I asked, confused. "It wasn't even like that. You think I'm dumb enough to bring a bitch in here for everyone too see?"

"I do. Why does my baby smell like next door? You had her watching my son?" India rolled her eyes at me.

"Yeah, I had to take care of something really quick."

"Oh, had to walk your bitch to the bus stop, huh?" she laughed.

India had gotten attitudes before, but this shit felt different. My chest burned. She was talking to me crazy. Usually, I met her where she was, but I just wanted to feel her. We hadn't made love in so long. If she could just feel me, maybe she'd go a little easier on me.

"Stop being like that Dia." I stroked her cheek.

Her neck ripped around like I was a white girl touching her hair without permission. "Rari, don't touch me." She shrugged me off of her.

I sat next to her, kissing her neck. It was her spot. It'd saved me so many times before. She allowed herself to fall into me. I slid my hands between her legs, and she parted them just a little for me to grab her pussy like the neck of a cat. She let out a small moan before thunder sounded off of nowhere.

Fucking Misiria. I forgot her ass was outside for a second.

"I'm sorry, baby. I miss us."

"I've always been about us, and you've always been about you. For the first time in a long time, my focus is where it should be, on Jelani and I. You need to go, Rari."

"Dia, why do you have to be so extra all the damn time. It's not that serious. I don't give a fuck what the nosey niggas tryna fuck you told you. You know I wasn't fucking around on you."

"Did you have a bitch in my house, Rari?"

I didn't know how to answer without lying or telling the truth. So, I said nothing. That only allowed her to make what she wanted from it.

"Exactly. Get out, Rari. Go stay with your mother. We'll talk when I come back from trick or treating. I'll call or something."

"Right." I said, turning to leave out of the back door.

I wasn't for the arguing. I had enough shit going on with this

Genie on my back. It wasn't clear how much of this shit was real. I felt like it was all in my head. I wasn't saying anything to her about my mother dying until I was sure this shit was real. It might all just be a bad dream.

"Rari!" India called out to me as I opened the door. "Where's his fucking costume?" she yelled, and I slammed the door behind me.

He was too young to be trick or treating any damn way. I tried to tell India and my mom that, but they weren't tryna hear it. Now, he wasn't going anywhere, and neither was she.

Rari didn't say a word the entire drive back to my house. I kept my eyes forward, focused on the road, too scared to take a glance at him. Although, I was dying to look at his face. I wasn't able to steal a glance until he sat on my sofa.

"Ready to make your last wish?" I asked him.

"I already told you. I'm not making no more wishes. Stop fucking asking me, man."

"Fine, we'll just sit here and waste each other's time." I huffed.

"You can make my last wish for me whenever you ready champ. Who's holding who up?" He turned on his back, head against the arm of the sofa, and right foot up against the couch pillows.

"You real comfortable on my shit."

"Bout to take a good ass nap. Hopefully, by the time I wake up, this Halloween shit is over with, and I can live my life," he yawned, closing his eyes.

I was ignoring him. My eyes were focus on the pages of the book I was reading. If it got to close to twelve, I'd make his wish for him but until then, I was waiting on him to tap out first. The silence wouldn't bother me. I could use some.

"What was your first wish?" he asked.

"I thought you were going to sleep?" I sucked my teeth, putting my book down on the coffee table.

"I can't sleep because I don't trust your ass," he sat up with one eye open.

I slapped him with one of the decorative pillows. "Erky."

"You ain't no walk in the park yourself, miss," he raised his eyebrows. "You gon' answer my question or not?"

"I wished for a boyfriend."

"And what was wrong with him?"

"Nothing. He was perfect."

"Something must've been wrong because the room all grey and cold now. What happened?"

"He was engaged to my best friend." I confessed.

Tears filled my eyes just thinking about it. The pain I felt in that moment was crushing onto my chest all over again.

"Damn."

"I described what I wanted down to the shape of his nose and I got exactly that; my best friend's man on the night before her wedding. He got too drunk, and his boys left him in the room with one of the strippers. He called me in a panic, not wanting to do anything to jeopardize his relationship. I went to save him. On the drive to his house, he confessed how in love with me he was. How he wanted me when we all met at the party, but my friend had approached him first. Then it happened. Car sex in the driveway of their home. Of course, my best friend was dropped off by the entire bridal party and we were caught with my pussy in his mouth." I shook my head.

I'd never had to tell that story out loud before. I didn't have to think about it often because once I became a G, none of it mattered. I was prepared for Rari to be disgusted by my action so when he burst into laughter, I twisted my lips in disbelief.

"Yo', you triflin' as fuck. Here I was thinking you Ms. Perfect and whole time you tryna be up under your best friend's man. Damn." He shook his head laughing.

"We can stop talking if all you're going to do is laugh at me," I rolled my eyes.

"My bad, my bad. What favor did you do for the Genie?"

"Do I get a turn at questions? I feel like I'm being interrogated."

"As you wish." He spread his arms, smiling. "But I don't know what you're going to ask when you know everything about me," he shrugged.

"Do you like me?" I asked.

I don't know how I built up the nerves to ask him, but I wanted to know. It's possible that I was imagining all of this, making small things into big things. But everything about our connection felt good. I wanted to keep feeling good when all of this was over. Regardless of how it ended. I wanted something to hold on to.

"I do," he nodded. "I don't know why, though. You've been making my life a living Hell."

"Way to ruin the moment, jerk." I hit him with the pillow again.

"I told you. I love my girl. I'm trying to avoid those moments but if India didn't exist, I'd have made you cum more times than you can count already."

I swallowed hard. My body heated in embarrassment and pleasure at the same time. The nigga was as smooth as a ride in a Ferrari. The fact that he had self-control made me want to fuck him more.

"She doesn't love you anymore," I confessed.

I don't know if I said it because I was his friend or I said it because I wanted him to jump in and act on these feelings with me. We only had a few hours left and Halloween would be over. We might not remember one another. I wanted to be in the now.

"I know." Rari confessed, running his hands down his face.

"Oh."

I thought I was revealing some big secret plot, but he wasn't moved. Of course, he knew. He was the one in love with her. If I could see it in the two seconds of laying eyes on her, he had to have known.

"I'm trying to fix it but—"

"Rari, please, please don't make that your last wish. Do not wish for her to fall back in love with you." I begged.

Rari put his head in hands, sighing.

"It's fucked up how you playing with me like this." He sat up. "This shit is hard as it is. Why are you making it harder, love?" he asked in his softest voice.

The intense stare he gave made me explain myself.

"It's not for selfish reasons. Not completely. I don't know what happens if y'all are not meant to be. I'm worried that it may break your heart beyond repair, if you aren't. I don't ever want to hurt you."

"What part of you could ever be selfish?" Rari asked, barely above a whisper.

"I don't know what this is, but I've never felt it. I like it. Whatever happens at the end of this, I don't want the last thing that happens between us to be me getting you back with a woman so underserving. She doesn't see your heart, but I do." I moved closer to him. "Every bruise, every scar, the little tears."

Rari's lips rushed mine and electricity shot through my body. He nibbled my top lip. I grabbed the sides of his face.

"Make love to me," I whispered against his lips.

I wanted so desperately to feel this man on top on me, in between my thighs, gripping my waist and everything else. It'd been too long since I let a man have me and there'd never been one as genuine as Rari. I needed it.

Rari pulled me atop his lap and caressed my ass as I wound my hips against the print through his jeans. We both felt his phone vibrate with a call and time stopped. Our lips parted and we stared into the other's eyes. Rari pulled his phone from his pocket, and we continued to stare at one another.

"Hello?"

"Rari, I've been calling your mom all day and she hasn't answered. You need to go check on her." I could hear India's loud ass voice through the phone.

Instantly my mood went sour. I climbed off of Rari and went to my fridge to pour myself a glass of wine. I made sure to slam my door. Damn, she fucked our moment up. It took most of the night for me to be that forward, just for her to call and knock me back ten steps. It was frustrating.

I ended up on the phone with India for twenty minutes. Fifteen of it was us arguing about shit that didn't even matter. Misiria hadn't made any noise since leaving me in the living room. I doubted she was sleep but I didn't want to wake her. Mostly, I was being a coward because I was scared to face her after ruining our moment like that.

I walked to her room door and tapped lightly figuring if she was sleep, no harm, no foul.

"What you want, clown."

I opened the door and stepped in. "My bad, yo'. Let me make it up to you." Her eyebrows raised. "With a drink." I clarified. "It's Halloween night. It's lit outside. Let's hit a bar."

"Oh, hell yeah. Maybe I can drink my attraction to you away." Misiria jumped up. "Get out so I can get dressed."

"Ha. You gon' need more than liquor, baby." I grabbed my dick, smiling before leaving her room.

I waited for her on the couch. One leg on the floor and the other hanging off the couch. I was more than a little comfortable.

She stepped out of the room a hood twenty minutes later. Misiria's shirt fell nicely, showing her ass but covering her pudge. She slid into a pair of Nike boots that she pulled from the closet. She threw on a jean jacket and applied some lip gloss before checking the mirror one last time. She looked good.

"Aight. You ready?" she asked.

"So, you do know how to dress? I was worried." I laughed, opening the door for her.

"Whatever. It's a bar not far from here," she led the way out of the apartment.

Walking to the bar, I caught a few smiles from passing couples. They must have thought we were together. I caught Misiria blushing a few times. We had to be glued together for the next few hours, I could give her something to remember.

I pulled her into me and wrapped my arm around her while we walked. The atmosphere went pink, and that rose smell returned.

"Oh, you like that, huh?" I smirked.

She shoved me, "Shut up."

Misiria grabbed my hand when I got my balance back and we walked into the bar. It was packed, all of the seats directly at the bar were full. She looked around for an empty table.

I leaned into her ear, knowing the music was too loud for her to hear me. "We don't really need a table. I'm tryna get my two step on." I walked to the bar, never letting her hand go.

"What you drinking?" I said into her in ear.

"I'll just have some wine. Red," she said into my ear.

"Wine? That's weak." I twisted my lips at her. "You gotta take at least one shot with me."

"Aight." She laughed.

I ordered two double shots of Casamigos. Shaw slapped me on the arm.

"You said one shot." She yelled into my ear.

"I got you." I wasn't sure if she could hear me, but she read my lips because she nodded her head.

The bartender passed me both shot glasses. I passed Misiria hers and downed mine right there at the bar. Her eyes went wide. I gave her a wink before sliding my glass across the counter.

She'd taken two sips and I led her to the dance floor. We danced through five songs with her ass against my dick. My liquor kicked in and I wanted to take her down right there.

"Let's get out of here." I whispered in her ear, before placing a kiss to the tip of her earlobe.

She looked up at me with a nod. "I have to pee first!"

She grabbed my hand and led us to the back where the restrooms were. I rested my back against the wall. She held on to my hand until she had no choice but to let go. She disappeared behind the bathroom doors.

My dick was throbbing. I was beginning to feel like a creep waiting outside of the women's restroom. I stepped off to the side and waited. I thought to go in there and get her because it didn't take that long to use the bathroom. She walked out just as I had the thought.

She looked around wildly for me and smiled wide when she noticed me. She walked over whispering in my ear. "I'm hungry."

"Me, too. Come on." I nodded towards the exit.

She grabbed my hand as we walked out.

"Damn, I forgot to pay. I be right back."

"Don't worry about it," she said, pulling me across the street.

Misiria snapped my fingers and instantly a fight broke out at the bar. It caused a panic and people came rushing out of the bar.

"Burgers?" I asked, pointing to a burger spot not too far away from where we stood.

"Perfect." Misiria might as well have been running.

"Damn, slow down."

"I'm starving. Come on," she whined.

I kept my pace, letting her walk ahead of me. The view was nice from behind. It was probably the liquor, but I was getting a softer, more relaxed, maybe even bubbly Misiria. Shit was nice. I was enjoying it while it lasted because I was dead ass about not making any more wishes.

We placed our orders and went to a booth. Shit was awkward now. Neither of us knew what the fuck we were supposed to be doing now. I broke the silence.

"So, what favor did you do for your Genie?"

"I saved him from a burning building on Halloween exactly seven years ago, today. I was coming from a track meet. I'll never forget it because for weeks everyone was talking about how I met my match. I mean we'd even gotten media attention and reporters were giving this Freshman my stamp. Ugh, I felt so disrespected. Game day comes and I dust this bitch. My team and I walked home from school amped up. We see this house on fire, a car in the driveway, a cat on the porch chilling, but no humans. So, I ran inside, dragged dude out and Boom. Three wishes later, here I am."

"You phony." I twisted my lips up at her.

"I swear," she raised her right hand high. "Turns out, Genie was trying to kill himself. It was his third attempt. He wanted out, but there's only one way out. The fire burned everything but him."

I hadn't even realized that she'd gone from victim to Genie. I knew there was more to these three wishes. She was holding back.

"What's the one way out?" I asked.

"I can't tell you that, yet." She gave a bitter smile.

"So, how'd you go from victim to Genie?"

"I can't answer that either."

"Yeah, I bet."

"Can we just be regular? Why do we have to talk about this shit. After you make your last voice, we can talk about everything."

I leaned into the table. She leaned in with me. Our lips almost touched. "I'm not making any more fucking wishes." I sat back in my seat and smiled at the waitress as she brought our food over.

"Anything else?" she asked, placing our plates in front of us.

"No, thank you." Misiria smiled at her as if she wasn't embarrassed.

"Actually, can I get a doggy bag?" I asked the waitress.

"Uh sure." She looked back and forth between me and Misiria.

I didn't give a fuck about none of that. I felt like I was on a leash, and she was taking her time giving me more rope. Like this shit was a game and she was making up the rules as we went along. I was done with this shit. Halloween needed to be the fuck over with.

I called myself protesting about leaving and Rari was getting out of his seat. I ended up tossing my fries into the bag and walking with my burger in my hand.

"Asshole."

"I'm the asshole?" Rari put his hand to his chest. "You the one playing games with my life, bruh. Picking and choosing what you can and can't say is bullshit."

"It is what it is." I bit into my burger.

I explained to him there was nothing I could do. I had rules to follow. It was frustrating having to explain myself over and over. He was like a big ass kid, upset about not getting his way. That was a turn off.

"Well, we on the same page because that's how I feel about your bullshit ass wish."

"It's 10:30. You really should make your wish," I shrugged.

"What, you deaf? I'm not doing that shit, fam. Go the fuck head." He cut his eyes at me.

"Fine. I'll do it. Someone else has to do everything for you, right? I might as well join the long ass list of people that do shit for Rari! Universe, give him what he desires so he can get the fuck away from me." I threw my bag of fries in his face.

"You ain't hurting nobody but yourself," he told me.

"Same, my nigga, same," I spat, rolling my eyes at him.

Since he didn't ask for anything specific, the universe would grant him whatever his heart desired most and hurt the worst. Stupid ass thought he was doing something, now he was about to be crying. He brought it on himself.

"Where are you walking to?" I asked, trying to catch up to him. "I want to go home."

"Yeah, well, me too. Looks like neither of us will be getting our way."

I watched him walk into a trail that was closed at this time of night. I didn't have a choose in following him, so I walked behind him into the trail. He found a bench to sit on in front of the water. As if it wasn't cold enough, the water would only make it colder.

"You would sit in the center of the bench." I shoved him over a little, taking a seat next to him on the bench.

"If you could just shut the fuck up for the rest of the night—"

"Excuse me?" I stood from the bench.

"I tried to talk to you inside the restaurant. You didn't want to talk. Now, I don't want to talk. Leave me the fuck alone. I'd like to wait on my pain in silence." Rari wouldn't even look at me.

If he wanted to wait in silence, that's exactly what he'd get. I looked for the closest streetlight that was near a bench and began moving in that direction. I hoped it was close enough for us to remain separated. I pulled my book from my bag and curled onto the bench. I didn't make it through a full page before his ass started talking to me.

"What was your first wish?"

"I'm sorry. Are you talking to me, sir?" I looked around in confusion.

"Yeah. I'm bored." He shrugged.

This nigga was a headache.

"I wished for more freedom. My father was strict while my mother was more lenient. So, my phone rang with my mother crying saying she and my dad were getting a divorce. Forty years down the drain."

"That's tough." Rari walked over to me. "Come on," he nodded his head towards the water. I took his hand, and we walked over, sitting on the grass.

The only thing nice about the water was the scene it created. The water itself was dirty and probably a resting place for missing bodies around the city. Still, it helped with the vibe. The moon reflected in the ripples of the water and a few fish splashed around here and there. That October breeze set everything off, right. I was beginning to wonder if I was making these moments up in my head or they were coming to us naturally.

"What's supposed to happen next?" he asked.

"Once your final wish is granted, I can answer all of your questions. But until then, we wait," I told him.

Rari nodded his head and exhaled. He wiped his asked down his face. "This the worst Halloween I've ever had."

I gave a soft smile. "I'm sorry." It was all I could offer because the night was only going to get worse. It was really just getting started.

We sat silently, both looking out at the water. I wondered if he felt as uneasy as I did about this last wish. On the outside, he looked calm. Like, he was prepared for whatever was coming his way.

"You nervous?" I asked.

"A little. It is what it is though," he shrugged.

"Well, what wish do you think was granted?"

Rari looked at me with knowing eyes. He didn't have to say

anything else. I knew it. He wanted India to be in love with him again. Silly me for thinking less than twenty-four hours with a man could make him like me. I wished he would've wished for anything else. I guess the heart wanted what the heart wanted. Even after all of my warnings, he did it anyway.

"Can I ask why?"

"Why, what?"

"Why are you so desperate to make her love you?"

"I think you cool as shit, but I have to try. If not for me, at least for my son." Rari gave me sincere eyes.

I shook my head, deciding not to press the issue any further. His decision had nothing to do with me and everything to do with his family. I couldn't be mad at that. It was a fucked up situation for the both of us.

Rari's phone rang and I looked to him. He was looking straight forward out to the water. I leaned over and kissed him on the lips, before grabbing his hand. His eyes closed, as he licked his lips and exhaled. I watched him dig in his pocket for his phone. I got a glance at his screen to see India was calling. My heart raced for Rari. Maybe he'd get what he wanted.

Rari cleared his throat. "Hello?"

"Rari, I don't know what happened!" India was so loud I could hear her. "He was here, and I turned around for two seconds and I don't know where he is. He's gone!" she cried out.

"Send me your location. I'm on my way." Rari told her, calm as ever.

My eyes watered, imagining the pain he must've felt hearing her cry like that. I almost felt bad for her myself. It was gut wrenching. My stomach turned with his.

"This is the part where you tell me none of this shit is real."

Rari looked to me with a straight face.

"It doesn't have to be." I told him.

"Misiria, if you fuck with me, no more riddles and half assed answers. Give me the real."

I nodded. "So, it can all be real. You start as a manager at McDonalds, you get your mom's inheritance, and India is in love with you again. You get exactly what you asked for, and live life as if this day never happened."

"Or what? What's the option where my son isn't harmed?" he barked at me then softened his eyes upon realizing he was yelling at me.

"You can switch places with me. Become a Genie, and it will be as if none of it happened, but you can't be a part of their world anymore."

Rari's mouth hung open and he ran his hands down his face. "This is the craziest shit."

"So, the wishes are real, but they give you what you truly desire. Your inheritance money was the only way you saw yourself having any real money. You wanted India to love you the way she did before Jelani came." I bit my lip, trying to explain it all to him. "You and India are not meant to be. Well, if it's just the two of you, it can work. But it won't work if you have kids."

That wasn't something I could see until his wish was answered. Once a wish was answered, I could see why they got what they got.

This was my least favorite part of the night. Rari would have to choose himself or me basically, they always chose themselves. They'd be hurt when their wishes brought the pain but when it came to choosing their fate, they chose to keep the life they wished for. Everyone was a selfish bastard. Me, too, even.

I could bring my family back, but I had to X myself out and become a Genie. Or I could live my life with everything I wished for. This was some sick shit.

"Look, I don't know what's going on between us but it's something. This decision is yours. You don't have to consider me I get it."

It never crossed my mind that switching places would mean she could be free. Be seen.

"How long do I have to make a decision?" I asked.

"Until 11:59."

We both looked down at our watches. Thirty minutes.

"What was your second wish?" I asked.

"Are you serious right now? It's not a game Rari. You have to make a decision."

"I already did," I told her. "Now, what was your second wish?"

Misiria looked at me with wide eyes. "I didn't make any more wishes. That's how I got stuck as a Genie. I didn't get the option to choose my fate. I literally got stuck."

"So, why did you keep forcing me to make my wishes? You could've made the last two and been free." I twisted my neck.

"I didn't want to force this on you."

"You bugging. I would've rushed to get them two wishes up off me to be free." I shook my head.

"I tried that the first three years. Then, I realized that it was selfish. That was how I ended up in this predicament to begin with. I wanted to be a good person. So much so, this year, I planned to stay in the house. I didn't want anyone doing me any favors. I was cool with being a G." She shrugged.

"So, you were going to do that shit forever, huh?"

"Yeah. Year after year of people choosing to keep the life they wish for, it gets frustrating. I felt like there weren't any good people left and I was tired of helping the selfish get what they wanted."

"I feel you."

"I don't mean you. I mean—"

"Nah. It's selfish as fuck," I nodded my head. "You don't gotta explain it."

"Yeah, so, I was quitting. Then your ride ass came along forcing a favor on me," she smiled. "I know this is your worse Halloween ever, but this was the best one I've had in a long time."

"It wasn't all bad." I ran my hand down her face.

She blushed, looking at her watch. "You're gonna have to tell me your decision soon."

"I know. But um, where are your parents now? Are they still together?"

"Yep. Same house and all. I stop by to see them from time to time. When I miss them, I just go to their neighborhood and watch their house like a creep," she laughed.

"That's definitely some stalker shit." I laughed with her.

"Sometimes they notice me, they toss a wave but that's all I ever get. I'm not sure how it all works. I don't know if I never existed for them, or they think I'm missing or what." She shrugged.

I looked down at my watch with three minutes to spare. "Well, now you get to find out," I told her.

"Huh?" She scrunched her face up.

"I'm taking your spot," I confessed.

Misiria leaped on top of me and kissed me with passion that could ignite a fire. Our tongues danced as we pulled our shirts off, then our pants.

Misiria sat on top of my dick, leaned in my ear, and whispered, "You're warming us up."

I realized I was changing the environment the way she had before. It was warm, red, and smelled like peaches.

"You're right. That shit is sexy as fuck," she bounced up and down on my dick.

I gripped her ass helping her lift her weight up and down. When she came on me, I rolled her over on her back and dug into her missionary style. I gripped a fistful of hair as I slid in and out of her. She spread her legs wide and pressed my lower back into her deeper as she worked her hips over the pressure.

"Can Genie's make babies?" I asked, not sure how much longer I could control myself.

"Let's find out." She bit my neck and did a pelvic squeeze that made me bust inside her. My body shook out of control. I'd never felt something so good before.

"You know." I panted. "It's a shame you never got an orgasm while being a G. The shit is amazing." I liked for my boxers.

"I said I didn't have sex." She slipped into her jeans. "I never said I didn't cum." She raised her eyebrows.

I could see Misiria the way she saw through me when she was a G. All of her pains, mistakes and secrets were on full blast in front of me. I wanted to love her, but the reality was, I wasn't even me no more. I was a fucking Genie, and she was free to go.

It was everything I hoped it would be. He fed my soul with them strokes, it felt like soul food, but for my pussy. A bitch was full.

"Aight, I guess I'll see you around." Rari kissed my cheek and began walking out of the trail.

"Huh? Where you gonna go?" I rushed to catch up with him.

"I don't know." He shrugged, still walking like he had somewhere to go.

"I know where you're going. Don't do it." I stopped walking and begged.

"I don't know what you're talking about."

"Rari, please. We can go back to my place. Figure this shit out, together. Did you forget that I used to be you? I can help."

"You free now, go live your life, shorty."

A couple walked by him, and the man brushed his shoulder. Not noticing him until he was right up on him. He didn't even bother to say excuse me.

When the couple made it to me, they smiled. Rari nodded his head, understanding what it felt like to be me all of those years. Meanwhile, I wanted to hide in my jean jacket. I'd gotten comfortable with no one noticing me, now that kind gesture of smiling, scared me.

"Rari." He stopped at the sound of my voice but didn't turn around. "If you're going to see your family to see if they remember you, or if everything is as it was, it's going to break your heart."

"I'll be aight. Thanks for everything, though." He tossed me the peace sign before dipping behind the corner.

I wanted to chase after him, but I knew firsthand that he had to see it to believe it. Hopefully, he knew my door was always open. My genie left me to figure the shit out for myself. I didn't have any help.

Against the advice I'd just given Rari, I wanted to see my parents. I didn't know what happened with me and my family once I wasn't the Genie anymore. But, I had to find out. I headed in the opposite direction of Rari. The closer I got to my parent's house, the harder my chest pounded. The wind blew, but I was sweating. When I made it to their block, I ran to the door. I knocked on the door as if my life was in danger.

"I don't think they're home, baby." A neighbor across the street called out to me, before walking into her house.

"Th—thank you." I smiled.

I tried the doorknob and it worked. I looked around, making sure no one was watching and walked in. I quickly shut the door behind me. I was overwhelmed with emotions looking at the house I used to walk into seven years ago. Everything was in the same spot I left it in. It was the same welcome mat at the door, the same sofa set, same placemats on the dining room table. It even smelled the same. I inhaled and a tear fell from my eye.

I headed for the steps to my bedroom and noticed the same photos on the wall, except I was in those pictures before. It was like someone had photoshopped me out and placed a new little girl there. She looked just like me, but the outfit was different than the one I wore in the original picture. Her ponytail hung to the left when mine hung to the right. Her dress was yellow and green while mine was red and white.

I climbed up the steps, holding tight to the railing. The steps creaked as they always had. I was anxious to see my bedroom, but I was also scared. I knew they had a daughter, but I always wondered if she was me.

I put my ear to the door to see if I could hear anyone; it was quiet. I turned the knob slowly, peeking in before barging into the room. It looked exactly the same. My red JBL speaker sat on the nightstand near my bed. I lifted the comforter on the bed to see that even my favorite sheets were on the bed.

The room was full of trophies from running track. My trophies, with my name. I opened the closet and saw my favorite hoodie. I pulled it from its hanger and shoved it into my bag. Another hoodie with the words DSU hung in the closet. She'd even gone to the same university I planned to go to.

I guess that was my answer. I entered some sort of alternate universe while another me lived my life. My parents didn't miss me because they still had me. They didn't need me. I ran to the kitchen looking for my mother's famous pineapple upside down cake. I only wanted a slice. There was a fresh untouched cake on the counter. I couldn't help but to grab a slice. I'm sure they'd notice but they'd blame it on someone that actually lived there. I wrapped the cake in a piece of foil and stuffed it inside of my bag with the hoodie.

I took one last look at the house I used to live in. When I was satisfied, I peeked through the blinds, making sure no one was watching. The coast was clear, and I snuck out as easily as I had snuck in.

I was closing their gate when their car pulled onto the block. I made eye contact with my father as he parked. Nothing, he didn't know who I was. I thought maybe once I was free from that Genie curse that everything would go back to normal. Wishful fucking thinking because neither of them had a clue. He walked over to my mom's side of the car and opened her door. I couldn't help but smile. My father was such a gentleman. My mother got out of the car and clung to my father's chest. They were both focused on me.

"Are you okay, honey?" my mother asked. "Do you need help?"

"I'm fine." I nodded, wiping the tears from my eyes. I gave a small smile before walking away.

It'd been so long since I'd heard my mother's voice. For so long I thought that if they could just notice me, hear my voice, they'd remember, but they didn't. I was just a weird ass girl they saw from time to time.

I left. There was nothing they could give me but a cell if they were scared enough to call the police. I should've never gone looking.

On the walk home, I promised myself that I would never go back. They were my old life, and I could never go back there. I could force myself in their presence and have some other type of relationship with them, but that'd hurt too much. It was time for me to move on. I'd gotten my freedom and was hopeful for what was waiting me on this new side of life.

I wanted Rari but it wasn't in the cards for me. I could meet a new man, make some new friends, maybe find a mentor that takes me under her wing and becomes a mother figure. It'd be a plus if she had a husband like my father. The sky was the limit. I earned my way out of that curse and was ready to live my life for me.

I didn't want to leave Misiria but I wasn't going to give her the opportunity to leave me first. She was free now. If I was her, I'd want to live my life to the fullest, make up for lost time. Add on the fact that I chose India over her, I wouldn't even blame her. I could use the help to figure this shit out, but I didn't want to be anyone's burden.

Other than the wild ass butt I bust earlier, I didn't feel any different. I was hungry and tired like any other night. The only thing different about tonight was that I missed my family. I was coming up on my mom's house and if she didn't know who the fuck I was, I wouldn't know how to handle it.

I tried to use my key and it didn't work. It wouldn't be her first time getting the locks changed because she was pissed with me. I didn't see her car out front, but I knocked anyway. I wasn't sure who I expected to answer or if I even wanted anyone to answer.

The door opened and I was looking at myself. Shit fucked my head up. I was stuck.

"I don't know what you want but whatever it is, it ain't here." Dude shut the door in my face.

He didn't see the resemblance. Misiria said that people only noticed her on Halloween. This had to be what she was talking about. They saw me but I wasn't important.

I knocked on the door again.

It swung open. "My nigga. I promise you, I am not in the

mood for this shit. Go the fuck about your business." He slammed the door in my face again.

I sat on the step refusing to leave until my mother showed. I waited about an hour before she showed up. She wasted no time going off.

"Lil boy, get off my steps. You don't see my no loitering sign? Go sell your drugs some here else." My mother yelled at me from her car window. She pointed me from her door.

"Mama, it's me. Rari."

"Oh, Lord. You not the dealer, you the user. You high as a kite. I got one son, and he is in the house. Get off my porch." She fanned her hand at me.

Damn. My mother was cold blooded. Misiria was right, again. That shit broke my heart. And my dumb ass wanted more because I was on my way home. I wanted to see my girl and my son. I guess technically she wasn't my girl anymore, but I did this shit for her.

India always talked about being a mother, more than she talked about home care aid. She took care of her grandfather when he was sick and was determined to help someone else's grandparents. Still, she wanted to be a mother first. If we could only be together without kids, then we couldn't be together. She'd given enough of her life to me. I wouldn't take that opportunity from her.

I grabbed a chicken box from one of the late-night spots. It would be a while before India left for work. I wasn't going to knock on the door for her. I learned my lesson when I knocked on my mother's door. I ate my food just staring at the house we used to share. Wasn't like I had shit else to do but wait.

I didn't realize I dozed off until I heard arguing coming from the apartment. I jumped up ready to save the day, only to see India walking out the door, cursing at the other Rari.

"You know what time I have to be to work. Why would you show up late? You so fucking selfish!" she yelled walking to her car.

The other me stood at the door with Jelani in his arms. That's all I really wanted. I wanted to see my son. I clowned Misiria for stalking her parents, but I knew why now. She just wanted to soothe the aching in her heart.

"I would've been in if you ain't put me out over that stupid shit! I said I overslept, my bad, damn!"

"It's always your bad, Rari. You can't do shit right," she got in the car, slamming the door.

I could see the look on his face. I knew exactly what he was feeling, like shit. A part of me wanted to save him. Warn him that things wouldn't get better between them so he could move on. But, it was something he would have to go through, so he'd never have to go through it again.

I walked off, heading nowhere in particular. I didn't know what to do with myself. Was my job real? Or was the job for the other Rari? Where was I supposed to live? I didn't know shit. I didn't have a choice but to go to Misiria.

It was embarrassing to have to go back to her to say she was right, yet again. Just the thought that she knew I would come begging, made my chest tight.

I knocked on the door, cowering to the side, not wanting her to see me through the peephole.

"In my seven years of being a Genie, no one had bothered to knock at my door except delivery workers. I've been human all of three hours and I'm over this shit already." I heard her fussing. "Who is it?" she asked.

I didn't say shit. I just knocked again. The door flew open and Misiria poked her neck out looking around.

"Rari," she held the door open for me to walk in.

"What's up?" I shut the door behind myself.

"What are you doing here? I didn't think I'd see you again, at least not this soon."

"I don't know what the fuck I'm doing out there." I ran my hand down my face, taking a seat on the couch.

"Mmhmm."

"You ain't got to rub it in." I twisted my neck.

"I'm sorry." Misiria put her hand over her mouth, trying to hold in her laughter. "I told you."

"You did." I shook my head.

"Well, don't feel too bad," she rubbed my thigh and my dick showed through my shorts. Her eyes bulged.

"My bad." I grabbed it. "What you mean though?" I scrunched my face.

"I went to see my parents."

"So, we already established that you were a stalker." I laughed and she pushed me.

"They weren't home. I tried the knob and the door opened." She put a couch pillow in between her legs. "I walked all through that house."

"Oh, it's official, you're a real stalker. That's crazy." I shook my head.

"Yeah." She exhaled. "I think I'm done, though." She stared at the pillow playing with the ruffles on the edges.

"Yeah, I don't see how you did that shit more than once. But eh, I'm sure I'll be back to lay eyes on my son." I shrugged.

"I laid eyes on me." Her eyes moved as she spoke. "I guess we're in some alternate universe or some shit. I don't know but I'm done looking back."

That helped me put two and two together with running into my other self. I'd always heard about alternate universe, but I didn't believe in them.

"Can I ask you something?"

"Anything." She adjusted on the couch, putting her hand on her chin.

"Was Misiria always your name?"

"No." She smiled digging in her bag. She pulled a trophy out and held it up for me to read. "Saniya Rae Logan," she spoke. "My Genie named me."

"So, you have to give me a name?" I raised my eyebrows.

"I guess so," she bit her lip.

"But only if you give me a new name, too. You know, to represent my newfound freedom and all." She shook her wrists showing her freedom.

"Bet. I already got mine," I told her, leaning back on the couch.

"Damn. You ain't even give me a chance." She held her mouth open in shock but laughing still.

"Gotta be quicker on your feet." I shrugged. "You wanna know your new name or not?" I side eyed her.

"Yeah," she nodded. "And it better not be ugly." She twisted her lips.

"Joy."

"I like it." She smiled at me.

"I like you," I looked up at her.

"I like you, too."

"You better." I pulled her on to my lap and kissed her.

"I think I got it," she pulled out of our kiss. "Gin."

"I think I fuck with it."

"Short for Genuine. You duck up but you're since. Your intentions are good, and your heart is pure."

"It's dope." I rubbed her ass and kissed on her breasts.

"So, what does all this mean like are we trying for a relationship?" She asked.

"I don't know. You free. I don't want to hold you back, for real. You wanna jump out of one pair of cuffs for another?"

I wanted her to say fuck that shit and take this chance with me. She got to see all my shit, and I was now seeing hers. I could love her. Like, the right way. This Genie shit allowed me to see what she needed. I could give her that, easy.

"Ain't nothing in them streets for me." She held my face and kissed my lips. "For the record, I like my cuffs in leather."

After how shit went down with India and I, I don't think I believed in soulmates anymore. I wasn't sure if two people were destined to be together, only destined to cross paths. I didn't know how all this shit worked but Joy saw the deepest, darkest, and brightest parts of me and was down for the ride.

I was able to see all of her shit now, too. We couldn't hide shit from each other. It couldn't get more real than that.

The following Halloween

"Happy Anniversary, baby!" I jumped in the bed, waking Gin up. We'd been together for a full year and besides a few arguments here and there, we were going strong. I didn't want to be anywhere else in the world.

"Happy anniversary." He rolled over, pulling me into his arms.

"You nervous about today?" I asked him.

"Not really," he shrugged.

This was his first time putting his Genie powers into effect. I was nervous for him but as always, he was pretending it was no big deal. That nonchalant shit got on my damn nerves.

"Well, if you stick to the plan, everything should work out fine."

"I've been thinking about that," he sat up. "I'm feeling like it's not a good idea."

"Huh? We talked about this. It's the perfect plan to get you out of being the Genie. You did a year, but that was nothing. When you're seven years in, like I was when I met you, you gone wish you had listened."

"Babe, I hear you. I was all for it, but now that the day is here. The shit don't feel right. Tricking someone into doing me a favor? That's the type of selfish shit that landed us both where we are right now."

"It's bad here?" I twisted my neck.

"You know that's not what I'm saying." He scrunched his lips up at me.

"You said, what you said, Gin."

"What I *said* was the intentions are not genuine. It's like we're trying to trick the system. I want this shit to be organic. All of it could backfire and then what?"

It made sense but I wasn't with it. Majority of our arguments consisted of him swearing that I was craving attention and me accusing him of being jealous because as the Genie, he went unnoticed. I was tired of that same argument. It was going to break us. Add on the fact that he refused to try for a baby.

He didn't know if our kid would be stuck as a Genie, or be half Genie and half human, if having a child as a Genie would keep him a Genie. There were too many unknowns for him. So, we were sort of stuck right here, until we made a move to ungenie his ass.

"You know I'm always right, Gin."

"Yeah, when you were the Genie. Now, I'm the Genie and the shit don't feel right. I'm going out here and if someone does me a favor, cool. But, if they don't, then we will try again next year."

"And if you get the favor organically?" I asked, wondering if he was talking about ditching the entire plan or just the first part.

"I'm not tricking them out of two wishes, Joy. I'm sorry, but I have to trust my gut on this."

"At least one of us trusts you." I folded my arms across my chest.

"Whatever, I'm getting in the shower."

Gin got out of the bed, and I sat there pouting. His dumb dog tried to get in the bed with us and I threw a pillow at his ass. It was supposed to be my dog, since he refused to give me a baby, but it was ugly, and I didn't want it. Well, whenever I was mad, it was his dog, and he could take the motherfucker back where he got it from.

I wanted to cry. It took us almost the full year to come up with a plan just for him to say he didn't want to do the shit anymore. I felt betrayed, played, and every other word with an ugly meaning. I wanted to fight. So, that's what I did. By the time he got out of the bathroom, I was at the door squaring up.

"Go sit your goofy ass down. I'm not fighting you." He pushed me and I fell backwards on the bed.

He had a towel wrapped around his waist. He opened it to dry his dick off. If I wasn't so pissed with him, I would've sat on it.

"Ugh!" I screamed.

"Re-fucking-lax. You bugging the fuck out right now."

"Because my entire life is tied up into some random person doing you a favor. Then, after they get their hearts desircs, we have to rely on them doing the right thing and taking your spot. People are not good, Gin." I smacked my hands together in his face. "It will take years for someone to agree to be a fucking Genie."

"Then, it just takes years," he shrugged.

"I want a family now. Not years from now." Tears threatened to spill from my eyes.

"I'm starting to think that we don't know each other that well. You doing a lot right now and the shit is not attractive. A grown ass woman having a temper tantrum." He shook his head at me in disgust.

Gin got dressed in silence, while I sat there, arms still folded, legs crossed at the ankles, trying my hardest not to cry.

Gin visited his son once a week. He wasn't making himself known to India or Jelani, but he went to lay eyes on him, faithfully. Sometimes he wouldn't come home until the next day because he was stalking his old house like a creep. I wanted to give him a son so he could let Jelani go. Yes, it was mostly selfishly motivated, but the other half of my motivation was for him. I wanted him to stop torturing himself with a son that would never know who he was. I could give him a son if he would let me.

"I'll be back."

"Soon, hopefully," I mumbled.

"As long as it takes."

"Long as you come back fully human, I don't give a fuck." I rolled my eyes.

"You realize this is real life, right? We have no idea what happens to us if I'm no longer the Genie. I'll remember you, but will you remember me?"

"Yes!"

"You don't know that. You've never seen it play out, so you have no idea what happens. I don't want to ungenie myself and you and every possibility of us, goes with it. I'm fine with staying the Genie if it means we stay together. If I'm not enough for you, you need to think about if you want this relationship at all, because truthfully, it might just be you and me. No kids, no family. Just us. That's all I need. Is it enough for you?"

I didn't give him an answer. It would be enough for me if he wasn't clinging so hard to his old life.

"Aight, I'm heading out. See you later," he said, as he left our bedroom.

When I heard the front door shut, I broke down into tears. I cried like the first night I cried as the Genie. I was cold, alone and had no idea what I was supposed to do. It felt like that very night all over again. I wanted to trust him, but I couldn't. I didn't want to keep going like this. I was going through with our plan, one way or the other.

I rushed out of the bed, threw some clothes on and headed out the front door. Gin and I always shared locations because we always felt like we could forget the other at any moment. I turned my location off while following him on foot. I knew exactly where he was going.

Once at the liquor store we met in, I watched him stand near the front door. A few people spoke to him, but no favors. I saw a black guy with glasses, and dress slacks that looked harmless, walking over to his car. He was parked right behind gin's car. I sped up to scare him and his beer spilled all over Gin's car. He rushed to clean up the mess and wa-lah, we had a Halloween victim thanks to me.

I swear to the universe that Joy was being a fucking headache. I picked the wrong damn name for her. I saw her force that man into doing me a favor. He was going as far to leave a note on my car.

"That's not necessary." I rushed across the street to the stranger in glasses.

"I'm so sorry. I can pay for the damage," he straightened his glasses.

"I'm serious. It's fine. Gin," I extended my hand out to him.

"Brandon," he shook my hand.

"Well, Brandon, you've just earned yourself three wishes."

"Excuse me?"

"This shit gone sound crazy but, I'm a Genie that only works on Halloween. It is 12:15 am," I looked down at my watch. "Officially Halloween. You did me a favor and as I'm sure you've heard no good deed goes unpunished. So," I rested my hands on his shoulder. "I owe you three wishes my man."

"No, thank you. I'm on my way in the house. I am a Christian man, and I don't celebrate the Devil. So, you can give my wishes or whatever to someone else."

"A Christian, huh?" I looked at the broken glass from the liquor bottles he broke on my car.

"Jesus drank wine," he gave a bitter smile.

"That he did. Welp, unfortunately, I am glued to you until

you make your wishes. Let's roll." I tapped the hood of his car, twice.

I walked over to the passenger and pulled the handle. It opened as if it belonged to me and I got into the passenger seat, shutting the door, and waiting for him.

"I'm not sure you heard me."

"I did. *You* not hearing *me.* It's out of my hands." I threw my arms up. "Three wishes, champ."

Brandon started his engine, shaking his head. "I have everything I need and what I don't have, God will provide. What do you want? Do you need money? I can get you money."

"I don't want anything but for you to make your wishes. We can have a long night, or a short night. It's all up to you, my man."

This Genie shit was easy. Dude was a little off but I was a genie so who was I to judge. Brandon started the engine and pulled off into traffic.

"Ugh. So, how does it work? I just tell you what I want, and that's it, you leave me alone?"

"Kinda, sorta. You make your wishes, and then you have one last decision to make, but I can't tell you that part until your wishes have been fulfilled."

"Ok. I guess I would like a new heart."

"Huh?" I asked.

"I need a new heart," he pushed his glasses up on his face. "I wasn't accepted on the transplant list because of my drinking. I need a new heart."

"I'm not sure if I can do that, but we'll see." I rolled my window down and stuck my head out of the window. "Aye, Universe, do your thing. Get my man Brandon here a new heart."

I wasn't sure if I had done it right, but I'd seen Joy do it enough times to give it a go.

"Can you stop yelling out of the window like a crazy person, please!" Brandon rolled my window back up.

"I'm just doing what you asked."

"I didn't ask for any of this, you forced it on me," he scoffed.

His phone chimed.

"That's probably your wish right there. That your email? Text? Open it up." I rubbed my hands together like I had money coming.

I knew the wishes were fucked up, but I couldn't hide my excitement. I'd been waiting a year to get my rocks off, and it has finally happened. I was a kid in a candy store.

"My email." He side-eyed me. He pulled over and parked.

"What are you doing?" I asked, confused.

"Pulling over, so I can read my email." He turned the car off before grabbing his phone.

This nigga was a whole square. Hopefully, it didn't take too much longer to get him up off my hands. I felt like I caught a good one on my first try. He might actually switch with me, willingly. Since he was a Jesus freak and all.

"Oh my Goodness." He looked back and forth between me and his phone. "I'm on the transplant list."

"You're welcome." I pat myself on the back.

"Fuck yes! I need a drink."

He turned the car on and pulled off into traffic without looking and ran into a man on a bike.

"Oh, God, no, no, no. Not again." He put his hands to his head.

"Again, you do this shit often. Your glasses don't work? Let me guess, they're for fashion?"

"Shut the fuck up!" He screamed at me.

"I think that's your heart, right there." I sat up to see the hood of the car.

"Lord, forgive me, I'm sorry," he mumbled.

I got out of the car to get a better look and was for certain that the guy he just hit, had his heart. I don't know, I could feel it or some shit. More importantly, I needed us out of here before the police came and he went to jail without making his last two wishes.

I opened the driver's door and urged him to get out. He was in a panic and refused to move. I pulled him out, opened the back door, and shoved him in. I got in the driver's seat and pulled off.

"I know that was bad, but I need you to pull it together or it's going to be a long night. You still have two wish—"

"You think I'm making another wish after that disaster? No fucking sir. Do what you got to do."

"Bet." I rolled the window down, while I sped in and out of traffic. "Universe, do your thug dizzle." I yelled out.

While I was not with tricking anyone out of their wishes, I was also not dumb enough to try and convince him to make his wishes. I wanted out of this curse as bad as Joy wanted me out, but I was going to follow the rules while doing it.

"What the fuck?" I look ahead of me to see a church on fire. "That your church, yo'?"

"Yeah." His breathing had finally gone normal, but he was holding his chest like he was about to have a heart attack.

"What the fuck did you want? What wish got granted?" I looked at him crazy.

I was all for doing my job but burning down churches was a no, no. Genie or not, I didn't want any blame for this shit.

"I really, really didn't want to go to church on Sunday," he grimaced, and I threw my arms up at the redlight.

I pulled into an alley and parked. "You are a sick individual. You know that?"

"Those who live in glass houses shouldn't throw stones. You just made me kill someone, so there's that."

"That was you and your heart. All I did was grant the wish. I'm ready to grant this third one and get the fuck way from your disastrous ass."

"I've already told you, I'm not making any more wishes." He pushed his glasses up.

"I'm not even sure I want you too, fam. You got a dark heart, my nigga." I shook my head. "But if you don't make it, I have to make it for you."

"Well, go ahead. I'm not interested. I just want this night over with. I need to get home."

"Same, my nigga, same." I got out of the car, and looked up to the sky, "Universe, spin the block for me one more time."

I didn't expect the night to go this fast. I told Joy all she had to do was trust me and the shit would work out. I couldn't wait to get home and prove her wrong for like the first time ever. Some wild shit happened, but it was a good night. I had this shit over with before daylight broke.

"Is this over with, yet? I just want to go home," Brandon said barely above a whisper.

We'd been sitting for over an hour and nothing. I had the patience, but Brandon was a weirdo. He hadn't so much as breathed too hard. The shit was making me uncomfortable. I wanted away from this nigga.

Smoke started coming from the car. It was crazy because the car wasn't even on.

"What was on your heart?" I glanced back at the weirdo in the backseat.

"To get away from you and get home. I really have to go!"

Flames spread through the hood of the car. "Oh, shit."

I rushed out of the car. "Have fun being the fucking Genie, nigga."

The car blew up in flames. I didn't bother to give another look to the car or Brandon. If the Genie switch worked right the flames wouldn't have killed him. If he did die in the fire, then I was still the Genie so fuck him. Plus, the man wasn't right in the head to begin with.

I all but ran home to get to Joy. I told her I could make this shit happen on the first try. The right way.

I walked in the house and Joy jumped straight in my arms.

"Baby! I was about to come after you." She kissed me. "Did you do it?"

"I did," I nodded my head with a smile.

"So, we can start our family?" she stared into my eyes.

"Facts." I grabbed her ass.

She hugged me and I lifted her into my arms and carried her into the bedroom.

The sun was starting to rise, and Gin hadn't come home yet. I was passed worried. I checked his location a million times and it said he was home. I assumed he left his phone, but I'd called it and couldn't find it anywhere. I was frustrated.

I'd gone through a bottle of wine and all that did was make me want to go looking for his ass, so I did.

I drove to his mom's house to see if he was there, he wasn't. I drove to India's to see if he was there, he wasn't. I went over to the liquor store, and he wasn't there either. But, at the corner there were news reporters, reporting a story.

"Good evening and thank you for tuning in. We are at the scene we reported about earlier this morning. Police searched the home of a man said to be responsible for several tragedy's that took place last night, one including a hit and run. In the basement of the home, they found two women who were rushed to the hospital for severe bruising in the vaginal area. It is suspected that the women are victims of sexual abuse."

No, no, no, no, no.

I pushed my way through the crowd. In the safety of my car, I searched Google for the news story being reported on. I needed to see the face of this man. It took about ten minutes to find any currently running stories. But Twitter showed me everything I needed.

I forced a favor from a very bad man. It had to be something in the rules against that.

A wind blew a sales paper on the windshield of my car.

You're in luck, we found some fucks for you to give.

What the fuck did that mean? That wasn't some random ass sales paper. That was directly from the universe. The sales paper blew over to the passenger window.

Two for one special with your vessel!

This shit was weird. My heart beat out of my chest, and I was scared to read anymore newspapers messages. I got out of the car. The wind was blowing wildly so I put my hood on my head and my hands in my pocket. I felt something and pulled it out to take a look. A fortune cookie. I didn't even eat Chinese food.

I wasn't reading that fortune and tossed it to the ground. The second I put my hand back in my pocket I felt another.

"I'm not reading that shit!" I yelled out to the sky.

My phone went off and I rushed to answer, hoping it was Gin.

You did not learn your lesson, you'll never get into heaven

Was in big bold letters on my screen. My hands began to shake from the fear. My stomach turned and my head ached.

"This shit didn't come with a rule book! How was I supposed to know?" I yelled.

My phone chimed again.

You weren't a good person, now your duties worsen.

Fuck that. I was not going back to that life. I ran around frantically, yelling to every person I passed.

"I'm here. They can see me. I'm not going back!" Not a single person reacted to me.

They couldn't see or hear me at all now. I stopped in the middle of the street and spun in a circle.

"Please!" I cried out. "I didn't know!"

My eyes burned, along with my throat. My chest tightened and my legs went weak. I fell to the ground and cried. I didn't know what else to do.

"Wow. I never thought this day would come." A slim man walked over to me with a toothpick. Someone is here to take my place."

I looked around and it was just us and the wind. I could see the wind in front of me.

"And what the fuck are you, exactly?" I wiped the tears from my eyes.

"You ever heard the saying, you reap what you sow?"

I nodded.

"I'm the reaper, baby." The man's grin made my stomach turn.

"Where's Gin?" I asked.

"Living the life you would've had if you didn't force that man into those wishes." He pouted, mocking me. "Alternate universe, where only bad luck exists. My job was to get good people, to do bad things. Sounds easy, right? Wrong as fuck. First, they're hard to find in this sea of trifling humans. Second, good people are just that, good. They are not swayed by money, desperation, or downright bad luck. They're always hopeful that everything will work out if they keep their hearts pure."

"So, if I'm a good person, why am I here?"

"You *were* a good person, but you helped a bad man do a very bad things for selfish reasons."

"I love Gin. I did it for us."

"No, no, no." He smiled. "That's just what you told yourself.

Eighty-one people died in that church. Assuming most were good, you have a big debt to pay, until someone takes your place. Balance, baby," he spit out his toothpick. "Enjoy."

The man walked off. I stared until he disappeared.

"Get out the street, bitch!" I looked behind me and a car was coming in my direction.

Just like that, people were moving around as if they'd been there the entire time.

"Move, bitch!" I was hit with a soda can, by a man on a bike trying to get by me.

I really fucked up this time.

THE END..

WANT TO INTERACT WITH T'ANN MARIE & HER TEAM? JOIN OUR READERS GROUPS ON FACEBOOK!

T'ANN MARIE PRESENTS: GRANDMA'S HOUSE | Facebook

T'ANN MARIE PRESENTS: GRANDMA'S HOUSE 2.0 | Facebook

WIN PRIZES, BE APART OF LIVE BOOK DISCUSSIONS & MORE!

WANT TO INTERACT WITH T'ANN MARIE & HER TEAM? JOIN OUR READERS GROUPS ON FACEBOOK!

T'ANN MARIE PRESENTS: GRANDMA'S HOUSE | Facebook

T'ANN MARIE PRESENTS: GRANDMA'S HOUSE 2.0 | Facebook

WIN PRIZES, BE APART OF LIVE BOOK DISCUSSIONS & MORE!